EARTHQUAKE

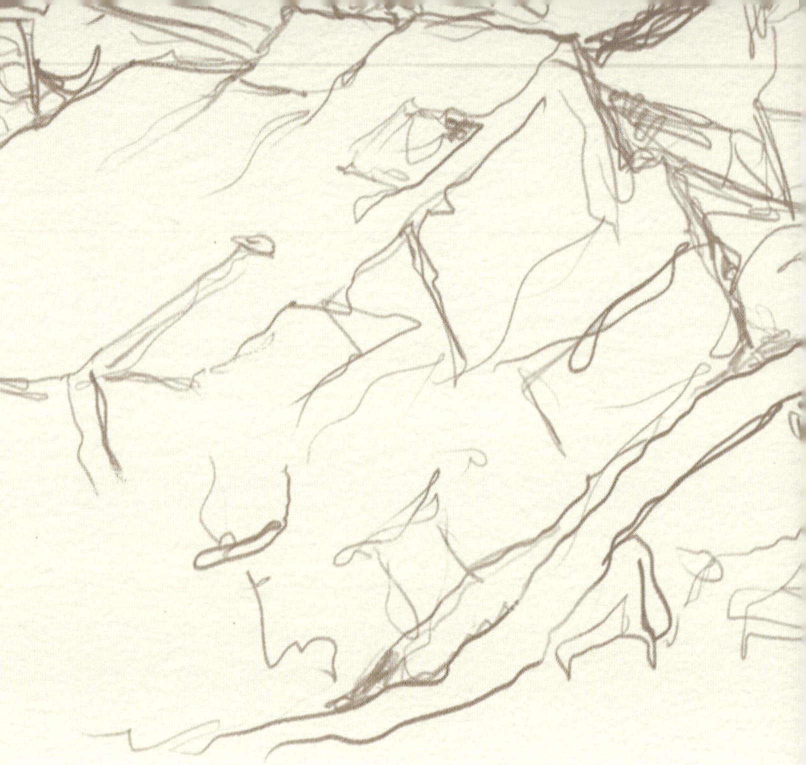

To Jack and Tom, with love—JF.

For Ellyn and Brett—BW.

Scholastic Press
An imprint of Scholastic Australia Pty Limited (ABN 11 000 614 577)
PO Box 579 Gosford NSW 2250
www.scholastic.com.au

Part of the Scholastic Group
Sydney • Auckland • New York • Toronto • London • Mexico City
New Delhi • Hong Kong • Buenos Aires • Puerto Rico

First published by Scholastic Australia in 2022.
This edition published in 2024.

A catalogue record for this book is available from the National Library of Australia

ISBN: 978-1-76152-495-0

Typeset in Morgen.

Book design by Nicole Stofberg.

Bruce Whatley created these illustrations digitally using Photoshop and Rebelle 3.

Printed in China by RR Donnelley.

Scholastic Australia's policy, in association with RR Donnelley, is to use papers that are renewable and made efficiently from wood grown in responsibly managed sources, so as to minimise its environmental footprint.

10 9 8 7 6 5 4 3 2 1 24 25 26 27 28 / 2

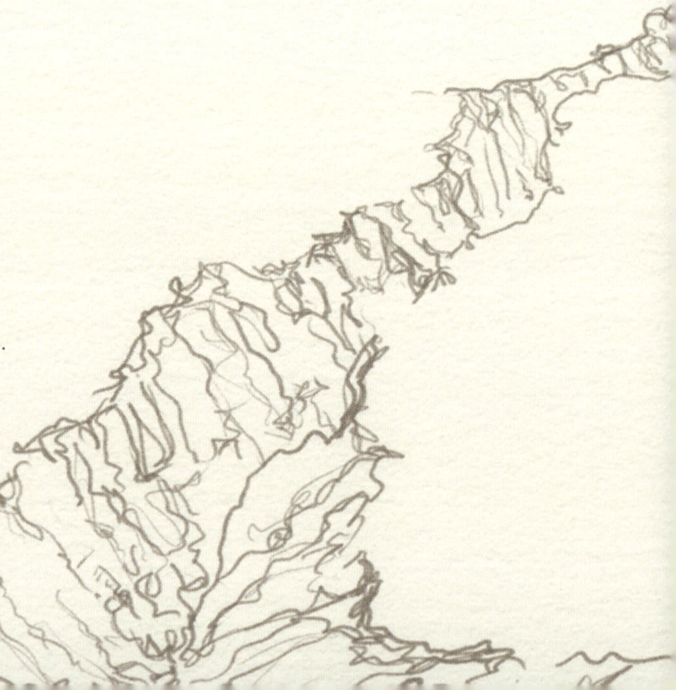

EARTHQUAKE

Jackie French Bruce Whatley

A Scholastic Press book from Scholastic Australia

‘I’ll tell you a story,’ my pa said,
as I snuggled warm in bed.
‘A true tale, this, me and my mate,
were trucking west in ’68 . . .

Then down below a giant woke,
the road before us shook and broke,

it ripped like paper, cracked like glass,
there was no way that we could pass.

A crazed, two metre giant's grin . . .

heaved the road so fast and high,
all we could see was dust and sky.

MECKERING
PUBLIC

Meckering's roofs and houses down,

smashed crockery that was once a town.

The railway line became a snake . . .

I saw how solid land could break.'

‘That’s quite enough,’ my mum told Pa.

‘Earthquakes happen far away.
No more talk of that today.’

...we care!
2
3
DRIVE

But then in 1989,
standing in the grocery line,

down below

the giant rumbled . . .

. . . all around us buildings crumbled.

Newcastle began to shake . . .

'Quake!' yelled someone. 'Out! Earthquake!'

The shop floor quivered like the sea,
walls crumbled, cans set free,
bouncing in weird jubilee.

MARKETS

In shock we stumbled out to see,
splintered glass, matchstick debris.
People lying on the ground,

screaming, crying all around . . .

That was the day the giant woke.
And on that day
my city broke.

But there's another tale to tell—
our quivering earth's a gift, as well.

Quakes are how our planet lives.
As ground sinks down, the earth then gives
new land, as mountains, islands lift.

Rock lies in beds that slide and shake . . .

there is no malice in a quake.

Mum was wrong, and Pa was right,
when he talked to me that night.
Earthquakes aren't just far away—
they may be here, perhaps today.

The Earth is large, and we are small,
but humans are the best of all
at adaptation—we can make,
walls that ride the biggest quake.

Earth may shudder, cities sway,
but we will all be safe today.

All our buildings can be safe . . .

once we accept

that Earth can shake.

JACKIE FRENCH

When I was a kid in the 1950s, we were told Australia didn't have earthquakes—till one rattled our school desks. Now scientists know that each year Australia has over 100 quakes measuring over 3 on the Richter Scale—the standard way of measuring earthquakes—and many more quakes that are almost too small to feel. Each level on the earthquake scale is 30 times more powerful than the previous level.

Earthquakes measuring over 5 on the Richter Scale happen in Australia about every two years, and the largest recorded quake was in 1988 at Tennant Creek in the Northern Territory, with an estimated magnitude of 6.6. Our land has the scattered remnants of 'fault scarps'—the features on the Earth's surface that look like large steps and are caused by the fault slipping. Fault scarps are places where the Earth has ripped apart more forcibly than we have ever measured. Any area can experience an earthquake, though major quakes are more likely in places with major faults.

Why do earthquakes happen? Because the Earth's crust is made up of floating 'tectonic plates' that collide with and slide past each other. Most deadly earthquakes occur at the edges of those plates. Australia isn't located on a plate edge, but the stress caused by our continent moving about 7 centimetres north-east each year means earth and rocks break under the strain and cause an earthquake.

This story is based on the unexpected and terrifying 1989 Newcastle earthquake, which measured 5.6 on the Richter Scale. It was the first major earthquake in a large Australian city. I've described the quake as residents told the story to me. Thirteen people were killed, at least 160 were injured, and over 1000 people lost their homes. The Newcastle earthquake caused A$4 billion worth of damage. It was most likely a natural earthquake, despite claims that it was caused by 200 years of coal mining in the area. But the damage and casualties were mostly due to poor local building codes, which didn't require old buildings to be strengthened or new ones made earthquake-resistant, even though the area was known for small earthquakes.

The likelihood of some earthquakes can be predicted, like the devastating quakes in the South Island of New Zealand. Geoscience Australia monitors patterns of small earthquakes caused by a build-up of tension in major faults which show that a major quake could happen at any time. The land beneath our feet can also be scanned for 'fault lines' that could move again.

We know far more about the Earth now than when I was a kid, but there is still so much more to learn about the mysteries of our planet.

BRUCE WHATLEY

Fortunately, I haven't experienced an earthquake first-hand, though I have felt tremors, which are scary enough. But I now have family in New Zealand where earthquakes and the tsunamis they can trigger are all too real. Though there are systems in place for such events, nothing could really prepare you for the devastation these disasters can wreak.

As always, I am constantly looking for new ways to illustrate and tell my visual narratives. Though *Earthquake* needed to follow the style of the previous disaster books, I wanted to see if I could achieve that digitally. Fortunately, I came across a program called Rebelle 3, which echoes the way watercolour flows and drips on paper. *Earthquake* was illustrated in Photoshop and Rebelle 3.